To Rob and George, with love
K.W.

For Helen
M.B.

Other titles in the *Imagine* series:
Imagine you are a Tiger
Imagine you are a Crocodile
Imagine you are an Orang-utan

Text copyright © Karen Wallace 1998
Illustrations copyright © Mike Bostock 1998

The right of Karen Wallace and Mike Bostock to be identified as
the author and illustrator of the Work has been asserted by them in
accordance with the Copyright, Designs and Patents Act 1988.

Published 1998 by Hodder Children's Books
A division of Hodder Headline plc
London NW1 3BH

10 9 8 7 6 5 4 3 2

ISBN   0340 67833X(PB)
0340 678321(HB)

Printed in Hong Kong

Imagine you are a DOLPHIN

Karen Wallace
Mike Bostock

Hodder
Children's
Books

A division of Hodder Headline plc

Imagine you are a dolphin,
Twirling, shiny in the water.
Others swim beside you,
Around you and underneath you.

A shiny dolphin sees his mother.
She swims beside her new baby.
If the baby wanders from her,
She drags his snout across the sand.

A shiny dolphin knows these lessons.
He's old enough to swim with others.
He's old enough to leave his mother.

Imagine you are a dolphin.
He roams the ocean like a seabird,
His skin is smooth like shiny satin.
He squeaks and whistles in the spray.

A dolphin dives into a canyon.
A shoal of fish flash past like shadows.
He herds them upwards like a sheep dog.
Other dolphins wait to catch them.

There are fish nets in the water.

The nets are death traps for a dolphin.

Some young dolphins leap inside them.

Other dolphins swim away.

Imagine you are a shiny dolphin, hesitating for a moment ...

A shiny dolphin hunts for flat fish.

He burrows through the gritty seabed.

A sand eel squirms.

He gulps it down.

A shiny dolphin rides the storm waves.
He rides the bow waves of huge ships.
He turns with others like torpedoes.
They whizz like bullets
through the spray.

Imagine you are a speeding dolphin.
He rolls and zigzags through the water.
He does not hear the killer whales
Who sneak like submarines towards him.

A frightened dolphin leaps and squeals.

He races through the icy water.

A friend beside him swims too slowly.

The killer whales are quick and hungry.

A dolphin dives. The others follow.
He dives towards a pearly shadow.
He's found their feast deep in the ocean.
A shoal of squid glow in the darkness.

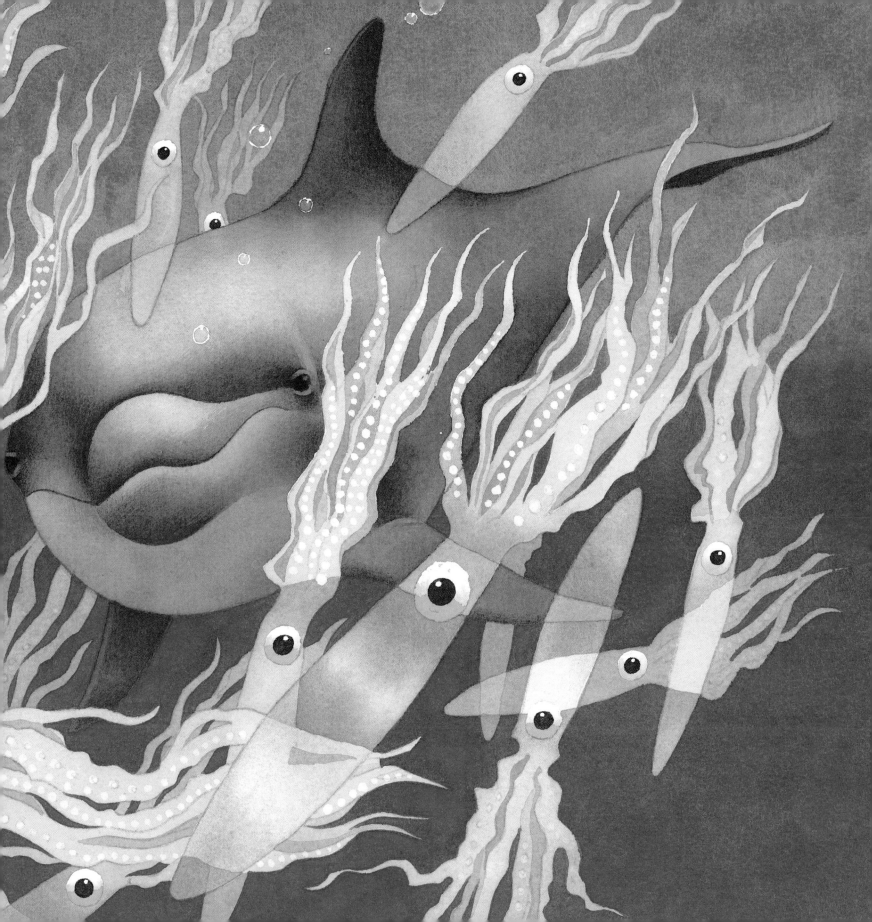

Imagine you are a shiny dolphin,
Full and joyful in the moonlight.
Other dolphins jump beside you.
They soar above the sparkling wave crests.
They play like children on the water.

Imagine You Are a Dolphin.